DEAR GOD,
IT'S ME—REBECCA

LARAINE BIRNIE

WESTBOW
PRESS®
A DIVISION OF THOMAS NELSON
& ZONDERVAN

WestBow Press books may be ordered through booksellers or by contacting:

WestBow Press
A Division of Thomas Nelson & Zondervan
1663 Liberty Drive
Bloomington, IN 47403
www.westbowpress.com
844-714-3454

ISBN: 979-8-3850-1823-9 (sc)
ISBN: 979-8-3850-1824-6 (hc)
ISBN: 979-8-3850-1822-2 (e)

Library of Congress Control Number: 2024902354

Print information available on the last page.

WestBow Press rev. date: 02/15/2024

To my beloved sister, LaVerne, with whom I share so much joy and laughter. And to my wonderful twin brothers, Lorne and Lyall, who were my best friends growing up. Bound together by our shared history, my siblings are a continued source of blessing to me today.

Contents

Chapter 1

REBECCA TALKS TO GOD ABOUT HER FEARS

Dear God,

It's me—Rebecca. Well, I expect you knew that already because you know everything, but I just wanted to introduce myself anyway. My mom says I am a chatterbox, so you can feel free to just read a little at a time if you are busy looking after other people.

I am so excited to write in my diary today. I am going to use it to write letters to you. Mom says it can be like a prayer journal. I got it for my birthday, and it has a red leather cover and a little gold lock with the tiniest gold key I have ever seen. I will have to find a place to hide the key so no one can read what I write. My mom says I would lose my head if it weren't attached.

Anyway, God, I really need help with my fear of my dark closet.

I know the Bible says in Isaiah 41:10, "So do not fear, for I am with you. I will strengthen you and help you."

You know that I don't usually have many fears. I love climbing trees and making them swing back and forth so I can reach over to the tree next to it. Once I crossed over six trees without touching the ground! I don't know if you noticed that because you were likely looking after something more important.

And remember that time, God, when I went with my dad to bring our two big horses back from the farm? They were huge workhorses called Belgians, and I was afraid I would fall off, so I chose the one that put its head down close to me because it seemed smaller. That was a long, bumpy ride with no saddle, but you helped me not to be afraid.

And I am not afraid of the dark when I play outside with my younger twin brothers (my sister being too young for that game). In fact, one of our favorite games is to lie on our stomachs on the grass and wait for the lights of a car to come down the road. We pretend that the car is a monster, and we lie flat and still in the grass so the beams from the headlights don't show where we are hiding.

Well, back to needing help with my fear of my dark closet. It all started the other night when I was sitting on the edge of my bed kicking off my pink fuzzy slippers. All of a sudden, two hands reached out from under the bed and grabbed my ankles. I was so scared that I shrieked out loud! But it was my brother who had hidden under my bed and was waiting for just the right moment to scare me. I know that you want us to love everyone, but sometimes it is hard to love my little brothers.

Anyway, ever since that time, I try to jump into my bed with a flying leap from my doorway. The problem is that now I see my whole room as scary, especially my closet. I always forget to close my closet door, and even when I am safe in bed, I keep imagining that there is a monster in there waiting to jump out.

I know in my head that there is really nothing scary in my closet as mostly it is full of my mom's dresses. Her closet isn't very big, and I don't have many clothes, so my mom hangs a lot of her dresses in my closet. But I just can't seem to stop the feeling that there is something scary in that closet. So, my prayer tonight is that you help me get over my fear of my dark closet.

Dear God, I can't believe you think that would be a

good idea! Keep the lights off and creep into my closet in the dark? I know that is the idea that you put into my head, but maybe you have another plan, like maybe my mom letting me keep the lights on.

I know Psalm 56:3 says, "When I am afraid I will trust in you."

Okay here goes.

I am putting on my slippers and tiptoeing over to my closet. I don't want to wake any sleeping monsters!

Now what?

Yikes! I am supposed to sit down on the floor of the dark closet and just wait?

Wait for what?

AAAGHHH! Something is touching my head!

Oh, it's only my mom's dresses.

Sigh. I'm still feeling scared.

Dum de dum dum. Maybe I will hum a little song.

Aggh! Something is tickling my head. Oh, it's just a scarf hanging down.

It's not very comfortable on this hard floor. I wish I had a mat to sit on. I should have brought my braided rug in here to sit on. My grandfather makes braided rugs out of old nylon stockings that have been dyed different colors.

They are lovely, and I like them better than the ones that he makes out of dyed twine as those as scratchy. But we usually put those twine ones outside the door so we can use them to wipe the mud off our feet.

Now I'm getting bored. But wait—I don't feel scared anymore. I guess it is not possible to feel bored and scared at the same time. Now I feel a little silly. It is just an old closet with dresses hanging down. Hey, God, that was so cool how, just by sitting here long enough, I don't feel scared anymore. That reminds me of verse 31 in Isaiah 40: "They that wait upon the Lord, they shall renew their strength." You gave me strength to overcome my fears. Now I can go to sleep without feeling afraid.

Chapter 2

REBECCA THANKS GOD FOR HIS HELP WHEN SHE WAS LOST

Dear God,

I have been meaning to thank you for helping me out when I got lost.

Actually, I didn't even realize that I was lost. It happened on one of our family driving trips. Even though Mom and Dad don't have a lot of money, they take us on vacation every July. We bring all our own food to save money. In fact, one time when we were crossing the border from our home in Canada to the USA, the guard looked down at the bags of potatoes and carrots in the trunk and asked my dad in astonishment, "What are you going to do with all that food?"

My dad replied, "We are going to eat it."

Our driving vacations are wonderful times because Mom and Dad really get along well when we travel, and Dad even shows me the maps and where we are going to go. The drives are long, and sometimes we need a rest. Dad made a plywood bench to fit over the hump in the floor of the backseat of the big old Pontiac so two of us could lie flat and the other one could stretch out on the actual seat. Unfortunately, there are only two window seats, so when we sit up, my brothers and I have to take turns being in the middle seat.

My dad always tells us to look out the windows in case we see something interesting, but it is mostly trees and other cars. Sometimes we play a game of travel bingo, which has green cards with little red plastic windows that you slide over if you see something on the card like a stop sign or a bridge.

The best part is arriving at the little cabin where we are going to stay for the night. My brothers and I race around checking the cabin out and seeing what we can find.

We feel so lucky if the little cabin is near a lake. Going for a swim while Mom cooks supper over the little Coleman stove is a special treat. The Coleman stove has only two burners, and it has a funny smell, but it heats up our food pretty fast.

But back to me getting lost.

We had been travelling to California, and we stopped to see the giant Redwood forest. We could even drive our car through one of the trees they were so huge. I can hardly believe that you made such beautiful trees, God.

Anyway, just before we got to the park grounds, we stopped at a garage to get gas and stretch our legs. I was wearing a one-piece jumpsuit with my special red leather belt, so when I went to the bathroom, I had to take the belt off. I hung it on the hook behind the door but forgot to put it back on again.

When we all piled out of the car at the Redwood forest, I noticed that I was missing my red belt.

I thought it would just be a short walk back to get it from the garage, so I told my brother where I was going. That was the brother whose mind was clearly elsewhere.

I set off walking briskly to where I thought the garage was. However, my sense of direction was off, and instead of retracing my steps back along the highway, I started walking in the opposite direction farther down the highway.

It seemed to me, after walking a while, that I should have reached the garage by then. But, of course, walking takes longer than driving in a car, so I pushed on a little farther. That was when I had the sense of you, God, telling me to stop and turn around and go back. I was disappointed, but I felt it was important to listen to that still, small voice in my head. I remembered the verse in Psalm 91:2: "I will say of the Lord, 'He is my refuge and my fortress, my God in whom I trust.'"

When I arrived back at the park, I found my parents very annoyed at me for leaving without letting them know. I pointed out that I had told my brother where I was going, but apparently, he had not told them. My poor parents thought I had been abducted by a stranger. They had been extremely worried, and when we got back into the car to continue our drive, things were pretty silent. Anyway, God, I just wanted to thank you for prompting me to turn around and go back before anything dangerous happened.

Chapter 3

Rebecca Talks to God about Winter

Dear God,

Well, this morning I have a question.

Why did you make winter? I guess you made it after Adam and Eve had to leave the Garden of Eden because you had to make them clothes to wear. Probably they didn't need clothes before that because it was always nice and warm. I guess they were not too pleased when they got cold. I don't like the cold either.

I know I should be thankful that my mom puts on my winter feather bed mattress and finds my bed socks. They are called bed socks because you only wear them in bed, so they don't have any heels. I think some lady forgot to knit heels when she was making socks and then decided to sell them as bed socks. And I am thankful for Skunky because I can put my feet on him when my hot water bottle gets cold. Skunky is actually a lady's fur collar made from skunk fur, but it is no longer attached to a coat. Maybe because it still has a faint skunk smell, whoever had the coat decided to take it off.

My grandpa (Pop) usually is the one to come and wake me up in the morning. He stands in my doorway and sings "Lazy Mary, will you get up, will you get up, will you get up? Lazy Mary, will you get up, will you get up today?"

I know the next verse, but I am not allowed to sing it. It goes "No, no, Mother, I won't get up, I won't get up, I won't get up. No, no, Mother, I won't get up. I won't get up today."

The problem is that, in winter, I have to leave my nice warm, cuddly featherbed and get up to get dressed. That is why I don't like winter. But I don't have a choice, so I grab my clothes and run into our little bathroom to get changed because it is too cold in my room. I crouch down in front of the heater under the sink and press my clothes against it to warm them up. It is a little cramped, but it beats trying to dress in my own room. I do have a heating vent in my room, but it is shared with Pop's room next door, so if he pushes the vent open on his side, then it closes on my side. Not a great invention from my point of view. The other problem is that, because my bed is a big double bed, it pushes right up against the vent so, even when it is open, not much warm air comes through.

I know the Bible talks a lot about being thankful. I was just reading in 1 Thessalonians 5:16–18 "Be joyful always; pray continually; give thanks in all circumstances, for this is God's will for you in Christ Jesus."

So, it seems that You want me to be thankful for winter! That is pretty hard, but I will try. I guess I can be thankful that it makes me enjoy summer even more.

Sometimes mornings seem rushed, God, and I don't have time to read my little Bible or talk to you for very long. But we can chat later. Psalm 121:4 says, "Indeed He who watches over Israel will neither slumber nor sleep." And that means us too.

Chapter 4

REBECCA TALKS TO GOD ABOUT FOOD

Dear God,

I do have one request for this morning. I know that in Ecclesiastics 9:7 it says, "Go, eat your food with gladness, and drink your wine with a joyful heart." And I really try to be glad. But it is easier to be glad when Mom makes the breakfast. It is usually oatmeal porridge, and she makes it best.

Mom's oatmeal is smooth, and when you pour the milk around the edge very carefully, the porridge floats to the surface of the bowl. Then I sprinkle it with brown sugar, and it is delicious.

I don't like it when Dad makes it. He cooks it without enough water, and it is all lumpy and chewy and hard to swallow. It is hard for me not to gag when I try to swallow it down. But no complaining is allowed, especially about food. "Waste not, want not," Mom and Dad always say. I know it says in John 6:12, "When they had all had enough to eat, he said to his disciples, 'Gather the pieces that are left over, let none be wasted.'" So, I know that Jesus didn't like wasting food either. Mom and Dad grew up in the Great Depression and always had enough to eat because they were on a farm, but still they believed in cleaning your plate. Dad's oatmeal was bad enough, but when he got on a kick of making Red River Cereal, things went from bad to worse. Red River Cereal looked like a variety of different seeds—like what you would feed to birds! It seemed to need a long cooking time so the seeds would get soft enough that you wouldn't feel like you were eating gravel, but when Dad made it, he never cooked it long enough, and we didn't have a choice. That's why I always look forward to breakfast on Sundays before we go to church. On those mornings, we get to eat Kellogg's Corn Flakes instead of the usual oatmeal. I find it so easy to be thankful for breakfast on Sunday mornings, God.

And thank you so much for inventing chocolate. I am a huge fan even though we don't have it that often.

Sometimes Mom might have a box of chocolates that we share—one each—especially if we have company. Mom puts the box back in the fridge where the chocolates turn hard and a little gray, but we know we can't just help ourselves.

On Easter, we get one large hollow chocolate Easter egg along with the neon-yellow-and-blue candy eggs that turn our lips the same color. Mom breaks the large chocolate egg into little pieces, and we all share a few pieces. I knew that eating a chocolate from the fridge was not allowed, so instead I thought I could use a knife and just slice off a little bit of the edge of the hard squares of baking chocolate that Mom keeps in the cupboard. I wondered if you wanted me to apologize for that, but Mom never mentioned it, so I guess I have been hoping that she didn't notice that the squares were a little smaller than normal. You made such delicious things, God, that it is hard to resist eating them.

Sometimes it seems as if I am always hungry. I wish I could say my mom was a good cook, but she really isn't.

She is great at baking bread and rolls and pies and cookies. There is always a tin of oatmeal cookies that we can snack on after school. We have pie sometimes on a

Sunday, but it has to be divided into seven pieces—three bigger pieces for Mom, Dad, and my grandpa (Pop) and four for the kids. Once for my birthday I asked my mom if I could have a whole pie all for myself, and she made me a rhubarb pie! I kept it in my bedroom in the top drawer of my chest of drawers. I cut off a little slice every day for over a week. Surprisingly, it didn't get moldy. It was one of the best birthday gifts I ever had. I even shared a little piece with my sister. Thank you, God, for my mom making me that pie.

But back to my mom's cooking. Summertime is great because we have a big garden and loads of fresh vegetables. But then we store potatoes and carrots in the cold part of the basement for winter, and Pop peels them up for supper.

Dear God, I try hard to eat some of the meat, but I just can't.

The fish sticks fried in a pan are soggy and taste like fish.

I don't mind fried bologna as it curls up in the pan. My favorite is fried Klik or Spam, so supper is okay when we have that. Anything else is so overcooked it is stringy and pretty tasteless. When I grow up, I am going to learn to be a good cook so maybe that is when my prayers will finally be answered.

I do like Mom's whole-wheat rolls, and once she thought it would be a good idea if I learned to make them. I thought I did a good job mixing them up and then rolling them into balls and baking them in the oven. When we had them for supper, they seemed pretty flat and doughy. My dad said he loved them, but my mom said, "How long did you let them rise?"

"Rise?" I said. "Ooops! I forgot that stage." My mom didn't tell me that I had to let them rise before baking. She said she figured I would know that given that they were always sitting in the window in the sun under a dish towel. But that didn't clue me in. I don't remember making dinner rolls again for a long time afterwards.

One of my brothers really didn't like peas, so he used to slide them under the table on a ledge hoping that our dog would eat them. Unfortunately, the dog didn't eat them, and Mom found out. My brother wasn't happy with the dog.

None of the adults complained about the food, and we learned not to as well. Mom would remind us of the children that were starving in Africa if we even hinted at not liking what was served.

One year it was funny because Pop's cousin from out West came for a visit and brought with him a big Mason jar of preserved citron thinking this would be a special treat for us all.

The little cubes of citrus fruit were preserved in a strong ginger liquid, and I could see that even Mom and Dad were having a hard time getting it down. Of course, Pop thought it was fine, but he has a cast iron stomach. One time my Mom was searching in the fridge for the home-made mayonnaise that she had made the day before for a salad. She asked Pop if he had seen the jar. He looked a little puzzled but then said that he thought that the "pudding" he had eaten for lunch had tasted a little odd.

Dear God, I do thank you for desserts and treats that make up for dinner not being the greatest. Oh, and thank you for peanut butter. I can eat peanut butter sandwiches every day and never get tired of them—just like my dad takes honey sandwiches in his lunch box to work every day. It wasn't really a regular lunch box with a rounded top. It was his metal mess kit from his time in the air force during World War Two. He kept his kit bag from that time as well as an extremely heavy white metal "smoke bomb" that somehow he carried back with him after the war ended as a souvenir. We were fascinated by the fact that he had an actual bomb in his workshop, although it got dropped on Mom's foot once and broke her toe. Dad never saw action because he was a nervous flyer and "washed out" of flying school. So, he remained a mechanic working on the planes and never went overseas. I am thankful that happened, God, because almost all the men in his original unit were killed and, had he gone overseas, my siblings and I would never have been born.

Chapter 5

REBECCA'S FAVORITE DAY IS SUNDAY

Dear God,

We prepare for Sunday by taking a bath on Saturday night. There is a saying "cleanliness is next to godliness," but I am not sure it is actually in the Bible. We don't want to waste the hot water, so we all take turns. I am glad that I get to take a bath first, and then my brothers, and finally Pop. I have never seen my mom take a bath. Somehow, she manages to take a bird bath in the bathroom sink and still smell fresh and clean with her lavender powder. By the time Pop takes his bath, there is not much hot water left, but he doesn't seem to care. He needs help washing his back, so he will ask me to do it. Eventually we are all ready for Sunday.

On Sunday, I get to wear my best dress, which is actually my only nice dress. My cousins in the United States have beautiful dresses, and their mom sends them to my mom when they grow out of them. Although one of the cousins is younger, I am pretty thin, so I can still fit the dresses.

I know that in Matthew 6:25 Jesus said, "Therefore I tell you, do not worry about your life what you will eat or drink, or about your body, what you will wear." And in verse 28 it says, "And why do you worry about clothes. See how the lilies of the field grow." I do get that, but sometimes it is nice to wear something special when we go to church. It's your house, and it feels polite to dress nicely even though I know you are everywhere and not just in churches.

I don't mind sitting in the pew on Sunday mornings. Our family sits in a long row on the left-hand side, three rows back from the front—well actually two rows back as the very front row doesn't have seats, just backs so people in the second row have a place to put their Bible and hymn books. Because there are seven of us, we fill the whole row. The children stay for the first part, and then we go downstairs for Sunday school. I am practicing memorizing my Bible verses. I have to learn quite a few plus the lines I need to repeat when I get confirmed. In our church, we get christened when we are babies, and then when we are older, we get confirmed, meaning we are joining the church. My Sunday school teacher tells us Bible stories with a big flannel board. The characters in the story are cut out of flannel so they stick to it and the teacher can move them around to tell the story. We have to use our imagination a lot, which is okay by me as I love imagining things. There aren't Bibles made especially for children. The first Bible that I saw that had pictures in it was a large, leather-covered book called *Hurlbutt's Story of the Bible*. It was written for children, and Mom reads it to us on rainy Sundays when we can't go outside.

Dear God, can you please make church more fun? My mom used to feed me Cheerios from a bag in her purse when I was very little so I wouldn't fidget, but I am too old for that now. The pews are also pretty uncomfortable to sit on. One church we visited had a "royal pew," which had nice soft, red cushions and back rests. It was the pew that the queen would sit in if she came for a visit. It had been years and years since she visited that church, but nobody sat there in the meantime. I wanted to sit there, but Mom and Dad wouldn't let me. It's not like the queen was going to use it, but rules are funny sometimes.

Yay! Today church was more fun as the adults decided to start a children's choir—well actually there weren't enough children, so we just sit in front of the adults in the choir loft. It's called a loft because it is up high behind the minister, but I guess you know that.

Anyway, now we can look down on all the people in the congregation, and it makes it so much more interesting. If I look closely, I can see Mr. Munn near the back closing his eyes. Sometimes his wife will notice and punch his arm, and he jolts awake. It is kind of funny to watch. He tries his best to stay awake, but he is not very successful.

Then there is Mrs. Crystal sitting proudly with her twin daughters. She always looks straight ahead at the minister, so she doesn't see that they are tickling each other and trying not to laugh. She thinks those twins are perfect, but she doesn't see them at school when they walk around with their noses in the air telling some poor girl that she smells bad. I don't think Christians are supposed to act like that. In Proverbs 16:18, it says, "Pride goes before destruction: a haughty spirit before a fall." So far, I haven't seen them fall, but maybe someday they will.

Then there is the piano player, Margaret, who sits by her boyfriend, Peter. She has a very frilly dress which she spreads out so wide that they can hold hands under it without anyone noticing it.

I am thankful that church is much more interesting now that I get to be in the choir. It can get pretty lively at times when we are learning a new song. Our choir leader, Mrs. Singer (great name for a choir director, isn't it?), has a lovely voice, and she tells us, "Worship the Lord with gladness; come before him with joyful songs." This is what it says in Psalm 100:2. Once during choir practice, she was getting frustrated with John as he was always flat, so she said that, for the real performance, he could just mouth the words and pretend to sing. He seemed okay to do that, but I would have been mortified.

I am so thankful that you made Sunday a day of rest. In Exodus 20:8 it says, "Remember the Sabbath day by keeping it holy."

Mom is good at following the Bible, and she won't let us do any work on Sunday, well except for doing dishes of course. But no cleaning of the house or weeding in the garden.

I know you don't want anyone working on Sunday because you rested on that day too.

I guess our dentist didn't read that part in his Bible. He was out mowing his lawn last Sunday, and it was a big deal. Everyone in the church was talking about it. He doesn't go to church, but his wife does, and she even sings in the choir, so she was probably embarrassed. The rules are pretty strict in our little church, but I don't think anybody was brave enough to tell him he shouldn't mow his lawn. The dentist, doctor, pharmacist, and banker are the important people in our town, and so people might be afraid to criticize them. I don't know if it is against the rules in the Bible to mow the lawn on a Sunday, so I guess I will ask you that when I get to heaven.

Chapter 6

REBECCA LOVES VISITING DAY

Sometimes on Sunday afternoons I get to go with Mom on her visits to the "elderly" as she calls the women she visits. Sometimes they are referred to as shut-ins, which I guess is a good way to describe them if they have trouble getting around. Visiting the shut-ins is something ladies in our church do on a regular basis. I like going on these visits with my mom because elderly ladies always have sweets. It is boring listening to them talk, but the desserts are so good I don't mind waiting. They always serve tea to my mom, but I am too young to drink tea, so I just get the cookies and cakes. Sometimes they make special things like upside down pineapple cake or raspberry squares. I am not allowed to ask for seconds, but usually the ladies will ask me, maybe because I am still pretty thin. The desserts make the waiting worthwhile.

Sunday is also the day that we get to go for a drive in the afternoon. Most of the time I hate going for a drive as the scenery is the same—short poplar trees and houses spaced far apart. Dad keeps saying, "Keep your eyes peeled. You never know what you might see." But I find it boring. The best part is when we end up at somebody's house. Sometimes it is my Aunt Rose's and sometimes it is my Aunt Mary's. Aunt Rose is a plump lady who bakes lovely desserts. When we end up at her house (sometimes at suppertime), she might just make sandwiches for supper. Mom and Dad don't think it is a problem to drop in unannounced on people when it is close to suppertime because they are fine with people dropping in on them. But there are no cousins my age at my Aunt Rose's house, so it is not very interesting.

But my Aunt Mary's house is the most exciting—not her actual house, which is pretty small, and you have to use an outhouse as they don't have an inside bathroom like we do.

But she has horses! I just love horses, God, and today you answered my prayer, and we ended up at her farmhouse. I know you must love animals too, God, because you made so many of them, and some are really funny looking. But horses are so sweet and have such soft muzzles, I could just spend the entire day petting their noses.

My Aunt Mary always looks tired and sad, and she has a hard life because her husband is often sick and can't help much on the farm. But whenever we visit her, she takes time to put a halter on old Star, the pony, so I can go for a ride. We are not allowed to use a saddle until we are much older as someone in our family (I am not sure who as it was a long time ago) got his foot stuck in the stirrup and was dragged and killed. So, we just ride bareback. I like to imagine that I am a great rider because I love horses so much, but I am really not. Star just walks very slowly out of the stable, and I ride her to the end of the pasture. But when I turn her around and she knows she is heading back to the stable, she starts to gallop. I have to hold on tightly to her mane, and then I have to duck my head because she runs right into the stable, and I would hit my head if I didn't duck. Riding Star is the best thing about visiting my Aunt Mary, and I think she understands how obsessed I am about horses, so she always takes time to give me a ride. I love my Aunt Mary, and I think she likes me too.

Sometimes I visit her on my own, and I tidy up and clean their kitchen and living room. Sometimes I pretend that I am like Martha in the Bible who ended up doing all the work while Mary just sat and listened to Jesus. I like helping my aunt clean up, and I told her it was because it was such a challenge. She just laughed, which was good as I realized later it could be taken as an insult. Sometimes I can just blurt out something without thinking how the other person might take it.

Chapter 7
REBECCA TALKS TO GOD ABOUT THE WAY SHE LOOKS

Dear God,

I hope it is okay to talk to you about how I look. I know the Bible says in 1 Peter 3:3, "Your beauty should not come from outward adornment, such as braided hair, and the wearing of gold jewelry and fine clothes." When I was little, I used to have nice straight hair, which my mom would braid, but I think she got tired of doing that, or maybe she read about braided hair in the Bible, so now I have to get a "Toni home permanent" as they call it. We go to my Aunt Mary's house, and she rolls up my hair in white plastic little rollers and then, while I hold a towel over my face, she pours this awful smelling stuff over my hair. Then I have to wait for about forty-five minutes, and then she rinses it out. When it is finished, I have tiny little spiral curls that make me look like I stuck my head in an electric socket. I hate how it looks, but my mom doesn't ask me what I would like. She gets the same thing done to her hair. I always wanted to have long, flowing hair, but as soon as the permanent starts to wear off and the curls get looser and look nicer, Mom says, "Time for another home permanent." My mom is a force to be reckoned with as they say. In fact, my dad often refers to my mom as "they" as in "I don't know what 'they' want to do."

There was only one time I loved my hair. I was visiting a neighbor whose daughter was a little younger than me, but her mom was a hairdresser, and she persuaded her mom to do my hair. She put it in long beautiful waves, and it looked great. But I don't think my mom liked it as I don't remember ever being allowed to visit that neighbor again. We just continued with my aunt as our hairdresser.

Anyway, with tight curls, glasses, pimples, and my mom being a teacher, I could tell I was not going to be popular. It would have helped if I had nicer clothes and shoes, but when I was younger, my mom just got me sturdy brown boots instead of fashionable shoes.

Dear God, I know the Bible says not to be envious,

and Exodus 20:17 lists "You shall not covet ..." as one of the Ten Commandments, but I would love to have a pair of black patent leather shoes with one strap instead of these ugly lace up brown boots! How can I feel like a girl without girl shoes? It wouldn't be so bad if everyone wore the same, but the popular girls in my class look really beautiful compared to me. There are twin girls, Cindy and Candy, and they have lovely black shiny shoes with silver buckles and cute dresses that most girls would only wear to a party. Plus, their hair is gorgeous. They have jet-black long hair and bangs, and their hair curls under at the ends. Sometimes they wear ribbons or bows in their hair. And they don't wear glasses or have pimples, and the boys are always hanging around their desks doing something silly to get their attention. No boys pay much attention to me.

Dear God, I didn't pay much attention to clothes when I was younger because everyone used to wear the same navy-blue tunic, but now everyone wears regular clothes to school.

One year all the popular girls were wearing big, full circle skirts. They would twirl around, and their skirts would make a big circle in the air, and then they would sit down on the grass and pretend to be flowers. I never had a big full skirt as my mom thought it was a waste of material, so I only had a tiny thin skirt. I couldn't twirl around in it, so the other girls told me I had to be a bud instead of a flower. Later when I was learning to sew, I decided to make a circle skirt for myself, but since it was a full circle, it took me forever to hem it with tiny stiches. Plus, I made the waist too small, so it was too tight to wear. I guess you were trying to teach me not to place so much importance on clothes weren't you, God?

My mom was a big help in not placing much emphasis on fashion. I only remember one time going shopping for clothes for Sunday school. Mom and I went into the city, and my mom chose a skirt and sweater top for me. The skirt was slim, which was okay as we were past playing bud and flowers at school. But the top was mustard yellow, which is my least favorite color. It was clearly my Mom's favorite color, and I don't remember having a choice. It was a nice outfit, but I vowed that I would never wear that color when I was old enough to buy my own clothes. At least my mom did agree to buy me a bra even though I didn't really need one. I just wanted to be like the other girls.

I told my mom that I hated having a flat chest and

looking younger than my age. She said that someday I would be glad that I looked younger. When we went bra shopping, we really couldn't find one small enough. It took us a long time, and when we finally met up with my dad, he said, "I guess you couldn't find one big enough, eh?" Sometimes his sense of humor is not great.

We ended up buying one that was way too big, but my mom got out her sewing machine and folded over the bust part and sewed it flat. At least now I have a bra. I tried stuffing some Kleenex in the cups at home, but the girls at school made fun of another girl who had "falsies," so I didn't dare wear that to school.

Dear God, I know I need your help in not being jealous of the other girls who have nicer clothes and hair and fill out their bras.

Chapter 8

REBECCA ASKS GOD FOR A BOYFRIEND

Dear God, it would be nice if a boy paid attention to me even just a little, although I know that is probably not an important thing to pray for when you have so many big problems to solve.

Wow, you answered that prayer right away! At school, a boy I really like passed me a note that was folded over, so I stuck it in my pencil case and didn't dare read it in class.

When I got home, I rushed up to my room and opened it. It said "I am going with you. Are you going with me?" (I guess he meant going steady).

I didn't want anyone to find the note and tease me (especially my brothers), so I took the note out into the forest behind our house and read it over and over. Then I put it under a rock to keep it safe. It was so romantic.

I felt so special after that even though I never actually talked to the boy after he gave me the note. And he was too shy to come and talk to me. But it was so exciting to know that someone paid attention to me. It's okay to have people pay attention to me, isn't it, God? My mom never tells me I am good at anything because she doesn't want me to get a "swelled head" whatever that means.

I tried to find the note a few weeks later, but it had rained, and all that was left was a soggy piece of paper. The writing was all washed out. But it was a lovely answer to prayer. Thank you, God.

Chapter 9

Rebecca Talks to God about Embarrassment

Dear God,

Sometimes life seems unfair. I had a crush on my English teacher all year. He was so cute with a dimple in his cheek, and he is a Christian and not married. I sit in the front row, so I get to see him up close. But yesterday he looked at me and asked me if my mother had seen my face that morning. I was puzzled until I realized that he was talking about my pimples. Then I was so embarrassed I could hardly speak. I have bad acne, but it seemed that he had only just noticed it and perhaps thought it was chicken pox. He insisted that I go to the room where my mom was teaching her class so she could check me out. My mom set him straight, and he never mentioned it again, but I was heartbroken as I had imagined that he liked me.

Sometimes I think life would be perfect if I didn't have to go to school. But I was reading Psalm 30:5: "Weeping may endure for a night, but rejoicing comes in the morning." I did feel a little better in the morning, so I know you keep your promises.

Chapter 10

REBECCA NEEDS HELP WITH BEING BULLIED

Dear God,

Sometimes it is really hard for me at school. Even when I was little, it seemed that I was often left out by the other girls. At recess, the popular girls used to play a horrible game. Two of them would stand in a huddle, whispering and looking over at the other girls and then whispering again. Then they would call over the other girls one by one to join them in a big circle where they would all drape their arms around each other like a football huddle, whisper, and make angry faces at the one girl left that they hadn't called over. They would do that until it was obvious that the other girl (usually me or one other girl) would be visibly upset and start to cry, and then they would all run over laughing and saying it was a big joke. I didn't like being the one left out, but I also didn't like being part of the big group that did it to someone else as it was really mean. When it was my turn to be left out, I just sat there and talked to you until the game was over. I know that, even when I don't seem to have any friends, you will always be there for me.

In Deuteronomy 31:6, it says, "Be strong and courageous. Do not be afraid or terrified because of them, for the Lord your God goes with you; He will never leave you nor forsake you."

I used to repeat that verse in my head when I was sitting there all alone.

I thought there wouldn't be so many bullies in junior high, but there are. Once one of the tough boys followed me home and called me bad names. I pretended that I didn't notice him, and eventually he left me alone. I told my mom that I wished he was dead, but she told me not to say things like that. Sorry for wishing that, God. Sometimes kids take it out on me if they don't like something that my mom (their teacher) does. I know she is really strict because she is that way with us as well. Another time, there was a boy who liked me, but I didn't like him. He decorated his bike with colorful streamers as if it was a wedding and rode beside me while I walked home. I was so embarrassed! The next day, when I told him I didn't like him, he walloped me with his book bag, and that was the end of that relationship.

It's not just boys who are bullies. In fact, the worst ones are the tough girls in my class. They all have older boyfriends in high school who smoke and drink and drive cars fast. The girls wear black leather jackets and red lipstick and do things like throw my school books on the floor and tell me to pick them up. They are always threatening to beat me up, and I think they likely would. It wouldn't help to tell my mom, as that would make it worse. I know in Luke 6:27 Jesus says, "Love your enemies, do good to those who hate you," but I really hate those girls.

I need help in trying to be polite to them even though they hate me too. Sometimes your commandments are really difficult to follow.

Can you please bring me even one friend so I won't feel so alone, God? A friend would help me take my mind off being bullied. I was reading in 1 Samuel 23 about how David and Jonathan were friends and how Jonathan stuck up for David and protected him even from his own father. It must have been so wonderful to have a friend like that.

Chapter 11

REBECCA THANKS GOD FOR A FRIEND

Dear God,

Thank you so much for sending me a friend today. Elaine just moved to our small town and started school this week. She is very shy and has bright red hair just like Anne of Green Gables.

She is not very pretty and doesn't have fancy clothes like the other girls, but she likes me. Now I have someone I can walk home from school with when my mom stays late at school to mark papers. Elaine lives in a little house near the train tracks, and she never invites me to go over to her house. I haven't invited her back to my house either, so we just talk when we walk home. I guess I could ask my mom if I could invite her back, but I think the answer will be no. I could tell by the look on my mom's face when I told her about Elaine that she didn't think that was a good idea. It's not like I have a lot of choices.

Elaine is really quiet and shy, so she gets picked on by the bullies just like me. I guess that is why we hang out together. I didn't think there was anyone more unpopular than I was, but I guess Elaine is now. It is nice to know that someone else gets how I feel at times because I don't really have any other friends. I was reading in Proverbs 18:24 "But there is a friend who sticks closer than a brother," and maybe Elaine and I will be friends like that.

Chapter 12

REBECCA TALKS TO GOD ABOUT TV

Dear God,

Are you okay with us watching TV? I haven't read anything in the Bible about watching TV because it wasn't invented back then. We don't have a TV because Mom thinks it is not a good idea. She wants us to read books instead. I found out that there was a TV show called *The Black Stallion*, and I really wanted to see it. I discovered that the twin girls who live right near the school have a TV, so I invited myself over to their house after school to watch it every week. We just sat in a dark living room watching the show, and then I went home. I don't remember doing anything else with the girls, as they were in my brothers' class at school, and they never came to my house. I guess I wasn't a very good friend to them. I am sorry, God.

Sometimes we do get to watch TV when we visit my Aunt Mary because they have a TV, and even Mom likes to watch the Ed Sullivan show on Sunday nights. Unfortunately, if we were watching another really interesting TV show, Mom would often announce it was time to go home, and we would miss the ending. Mom really isn't tuned in to what kids want.

Some people think that watching TV is wrong, but some of the shows are really interesting.

I did get to watch TV when I was babysitting our neighbor's children. The parents would stay out really late, and I would watch TV after I cleaned up the kitchen. But once my brothers got old enough to babysit, the parents asked them instead of me because my brothers would do it cheaper. I remember watching a detective show called *Peter Gunn*, which starred Craig Stevens. He was so handsome just like Vince Edwards who played Ben Casey. I always loved shows about doctors and nurses.

Chapter 13

REBECCA LEARNS THE PITFALLS OF LYING

Dear God,

I know Ephesians 4:15 says, "Instead, speaking the truth in love" because you don't want us to lie, but sometimes it is really hard. I love to read, and just when I am getting to an interesting part of the story, my mom comes in and turns off my light. Last night after she did that, I got out my little red flashlight and read my book under the covers.

I heard her coming up to check, and I quickly switched off the light. I closed my eyes and tried to breathe normally, but she knew I was still awake and said, "Have you been reading under the covers?"

"No," I said, and I turned over quickly to face the wall.

She went back downstairs, but I started to feel really badly that I had lied to her.

I knew that You would want me to tell the truth because I had that uncomfortable feeling in my stomach.

So I went downstairs to the kitchen and said, "I'm sorry. I was reading, and I lied to you."

I thought I would get in trouble, but she just said, "That's good that you told the truth."

But you taught me a really hard lesson about lying, God. I know I should have been content with having a secret boyfriend (the one who wrote me the note when I was younger), but I couldn't tell anyone about that, and all the other girls were talking about their boyfriends.

I didn't want to feel left out, so I decided to invent a boyfriend. Friends of my parents had a son who was really nice and very good looking, and no one in my class had ever met him, so I told the girls in my class that he was my boyfriend. I didn't realize that word would get back to the boy himself. The next time his family came to visit, I was playing catch with him in the front yard. When he threw the ball to me, he said, "Who is your boyfriend?" in a teasing manner.

Dear God, I was so mortified I wished that the earth

could have swallowed me up! I know I turned red, and I probably ran away.

Now I know why in, Ephesians 4:25, the Bible says, "Therefore each of you must put off falsehood and speak truthfully to his neighbor." It is terrible to be found out, and now I can't even think about speaking to that boy again much less enjoy hanging out with him. That was a really hard lesson to learn.

Chapter 14

REBECCA TALKS TO GOD ABOUT BEING OVERLOOKED

Dear God,

Sometimes I feel angry at my mom when she acts as if she is the helpful one and not me.

Once I found a woman's paycheck in the snow near the bank. I gave it to my mom, and then we saw a woman looking for it. She wasn't dressed very well, and it looked like she really needed the money. My mom called her over to the car and handed her the check. She was so happy and kept saying thank you to my mom over and over. My mom never said that I was the one who found the check, and I was angry. I know Matthew 6:3 says, "But when you give to the needy do not let your left hand know what your right hand is doing so that your giving may be in secret," but I think my mom was being selfish taking all the credit for herself and not mentioning me at all. But I couldn't say anything to her, or she would have been really angry. I know that you were happy that I found the woman's check, but sometimes it is nice for other people to tell me that too. You must feel overlooked that way sometimes, too, when people don't say thank you to you, especially when it is a wonderful answer to prayer like healing their illnesses. Some people who don't know you just say it was "luck" or a "coincidence," but I know it was really you blessing them.

Chapter 15

REBECCA NEEDS TO HAVE COURAGE AT THE DOCTOR'S OFFICE

Dear God,

Thank you for giving me courage when I had to go to the doctor. I had an abscess on my stomach that wouldn't go away, and it was hurting quite a lot. My mom took me to our doctor, but I went into the room by myself. He wasn't very gentle and told me he would have to lance it to drain the pus.

He took out what to me looked exactly like my protractor from my math set with one blunt end and one sharp end. Then he stuck the needle end into the abscess, and that really hurt. But you helped me not to cry, God, because I didn't want to seem like a baby. I remembered the verse in Psalm 56:3: "When I am afraid I will trust in You." I am glad that I memorized a lot of Bible verses because they really help when I am in a difficult situation.

The only other time I got hurt was when my brothers and I were swimming in our pond and there was so much water that it overflowed into the ditch. We were swimming along in the ditch, but someone had thrown broken beer bottles into it, and one of my brothers cut his toe, and I got a big cut down the front of my leg, which needed stiches. Later my mom said that they didn't realize that my brother's cut was worse because I was making such a big fuss. Thank you for looking after both of us that time.

Speaking of swimming, one Sunday afternoon, I was swimming with my sister and younger cousin, and we were playing around the dock. I was showing them how you could hold your breath, then swim under the dock and pop up underneath it where there was an air pocket. When they tried it, one of them was still holding the outside edge of the dock with one hand and so my mom and aunt thought she was drowning and rushed in with their clothes on to save her. I swam off across the lake, and my sister and cousin got a scolding. Oh dear, that was another time I wasn't very nice to my sister. It is good that she forgives me when I am thoughtless.

Chapter 16

REBECCA IS THANKFUL TO GOD FOR MUSIC

Dear God,

I want to thank you for making music. The first song that I learned was "Jesus Loves Me." We learned other songs in Sunday school too like "This Little Light of Mine" and "I'll Be a Sunbeam for Jesus" and "Jesus Loves the Little Children." I love singing. When we are singing and playing music, everyone in our family can enjoy being together. My dad plays the accordion and the fiddle. One of my brothers plays the guitar, the other plays the fiddle, and I play the piano. Music is so wonderful when times are tough because it always cheers everyone up. It was one of the best ideas that you ever had!

I love so many different kinds of music—classical

music, fiddle music, Scottish and Irish music, but not jazz or country music. Our heritage is Scottish, Irish, and English, and my mom loves English folk songs. Dad likes the Scottish and Irish songs, so we have lots to choose from. Sometimes when I hear someone sing "Scotland the Brave," I get emotional, and when I hear bagpipes playing, I can feel the tears coming - it is so beautiful.

Both Dad and Pop like me to chord for them on the piano while they play the fiddle. If I chord for Pop, then I will make time to chord for Dad as well. They both play by ear and have probably a hundred songs that they know from memory. I have my favorites, and Pop always plays those because he knows I like them. I love the music of "One Hundred Pipers" and the fast pace of "The Devil's Dream."

It's okay if I like that one, right? I don't spend much time thinking about the devil, and it's just a song, so I hope you are okay that it is one of my favorites. There is another song called. "Little Brown Jug," which must be about alcohol because Mom frowns when Dad plays that song.

I know you must love music too because there are so many verses in the Bible about praising you with musical instruments.

I am learning to play some songs on the piano like "When the Saints Go Marching In" and "Swing Low, Sweet Chariot." My favorite gospel song is "The Battle Hymn of the Republic," and that brings tears to my eyes as well. "Amazing Grace" is also one of my favorite songs, and I am learning to play it on the piano too.

Dear God, even though I love music, I wish I didn't have to practice the piano so much every day, especially the scales and chords and arpeggios.

My piano teacher is married to my dad's cousin, and she is okay but not a wonderful musician herself. In fact, my dad always wonders why she can't play "O Canada" without the music. Dad doesn't really understand that some people can play by ear (like most of our family) and others need to have the music in front of them all the time. He is very puzzled that our music teacher can't play the piano without reading the music from a sheet of paper, and he keeps talking about it every opportunity he gets. He says it with the same astonished tone of voice he'd use if he were saying she can't walk despite having two good legs. Anyway, she is the only piano teacher in town, so there is not much choice. I do love music, and most of the time I don't mind practicing. Our teacher comes to our house because my brothers and I all take lessons. Once I had been playing with my pet rat, and I was carrying him around on my shoulder when I went into the living room for my piano lesson. My teacher really freaked out. Sniffy wouldn't hurt anyone, but he is pretty big and has a long pink tail that looks like a file, so I guess she was a little frightened.

Chapter 17

Rebecca Loves Animals

Dear God,

Speaking of Sniffy, my rat, I was so pleased when I ended up winning him in a contest. Remember I prayed to you that I would win? We had two white Norway rats at school for an experiment about nutrition. One was fed leafy greens and the other was fed just white bread, and after a few months, it was clear that the one who was fed more nutritious food was much healthier than the other one. Anyway, after the experiment was over, the teacher announced a contest. She said that whoever brought in the best cage could take home the healthy rat. I was so excited, and I asked Pop if he would help me make a cage. We made one out of an old orange crate and put a little water dish and some wood shavings in it. It turned out that I won the prize, so I got to take Sniffy home with me. I don't remember if other kids brought in cages or not. Maybe their parents weren't as keen about rats.

Sniffy was pretty good, except one time I let him sleep by my feet in my bed at night, and he chewed the end of my white sheet into shreds. Mom had to sew it up, and there were dozens of rows of machine stitching going back and forth to repair the part that he had chewed. After that, he had to sleep in his cage. I made the mistake of letting him out of his cage once when I had him outside, and he escaped into the bush.

I don't know if he survived. Being a Norway rat, maybe he would adapt to a harsh climate. I hope so anyway. He was so cute, and I loved the way his whiskers moved when he was eating.

Thank you so much for our dog, Ginger. He is the cutest thing. He looks like an Irish setter, only he has short stubby legs. He might be a cocker spaniel, but he has a long fluffy tail. He is not allowed to come into the dining room or living room; he has to stay in the kitchen or laundry room. He knows the rules but tries to stretch them. He will lie with his nose just over the boundary between the kitchen and dining room hoping he will be allowed to join us. He takes off from the house most days and walks along the road to visit our neighbors. Often, they will give him treats, and then afterwards he will return home. Sometimes we see him standing at the end of our driveway looking back to see if we notice him trying to head out. If no one notices and no one calls him back, he will quietly sneak off.

He is good company for Pop when the rest of us go on vacation. One time we were all driving in the car going somewhere and we saw he was in the ditch and not moving much. He had been hit by a car, and he couldn't move his back legs.

I was praying so hard, God, that you would save him because my dad thought he should be put down so he wouldn't suffer.

But I begged my parents to let me look after him, and we put him in the basement by the furnace in a little bed. Gradually he got better and was able to walk again. Despite his accident, he never stopped going down the road to visit his friends. Thank you, God, for saving his life as I would have been heartbroken to lose him.

I hope there are going to be animals in Heaven. Isaiah 11:6 says, "The wolf will live with the lamb. The leopard will lie down with the goat." So it sounds as if there will be animals, but they won't be fighting and eating each other. That will be wonderful.

When I was younger, we had chickens that lived in a long hen house and gave us eggs. When I carried my empty milk bottle home after school, I would catch grasshoppers and put them in the bottle. Then I would feed them to the chickens for a bit of variety in their diet. But chickens are pretty silly, and I never had one for a pet.

Then there were our cattle. My dad loved Black Angus cattle, and he hoped that he could raise them on the eighty acres just behind our house. Unfortunately, it was just scrub land and pretty wet one year, so they all got something weird called foot rot, which he tried to treat by putting a white powder on their hooves. But they all got sick, and he had to sell them.

When we did have the cattle, sometimes it would be fun to pretend to hunt them. We had broken hockey sticks for spears, and sometimes we tried to throw our spears at them. One time one of the cows looked at us and started to come closer, so we quickly climbed a tree in case it charged. My brothers and I also played with bows and arrows that we made out of flexible willow branches and twine. Mom didn't want to encourage my brothers to be cowboys with pretend guns, so we just adapted and played Indians instead with our bows and arrows.

I know one of the commandments in Exodus 20:13 is "Thou shalt not murder." Thank you, God, that my dad doesn't believe in shooting animals. He is softhearted and doesn't even shoot ducks unless it is for food. But he really doesn't like crows and the damage they do driving off the other birds and eating the corn. So he has a twenty-two rifle in his shop attached to the garage. One day, I took the gun, and my little sister and I went looking for crows. I don't think my mom noticed that we were gone. Anyway, I shot a crow out of the tree, and it was on the ground, not moving. I told my little sister to take a stick and poke it to see if it was dead. When she touched it with the stick, it flapped its wings and up came its head. She was so scared, and I realized afterwards that it was really not a nice thing to ask her to do. My brothers and I were such dare devils that we didn't realize how traumatic it must have been for her. We used to climb up on the roof of the hen house and jump from it to the roof of a small shed. She was nervous to do it, so we tied a rope around her waist, jumped over to the shed roof, and told her to jump and we would catch her if she fell. Dear God, can you please help me to be a better sister?

Chapter 18

REBECCA ASKS GOD TO HELP HER WITH HER FAMILY

Dear God,

I know in Exodus 20:12 it says, "Honor your father and mother," and I really try to do that. Sometimes it is hard because I don't remember my mom or dad ever saying that they loved me, but really nobody in our family says things like that. I guess you knew that sometimes it would be hard to love our parents so you put "Honor your father and mother" instead of "Love your father and mother" in the Ten Commandments. Honor means respect, and I do respect my parents although I can't say I really love them.

Once I tried to get my mom to say something nice to me by asking her "Who do you think is my favorite person?" I was hoping she would guess that she was one of my favorite people and maybe tell me that I was one of her favorite people. She didn't really understand what I was asking and guessed my aunt. I am so glad, God, that you always understand what I say, because we don't have very good communication in my family.

Can you please make my mom and dad get along better? My mom is really the boss, and dad just goes along with what she wants. My dad likes to putter in his shop making or repairing things. He is really smart, but he didn't finish high school. He reads the newspaper and the *Readers Digest*. My mom finished high school and went to normal school which is what they called teachers college back then, so she has more education than my dad and has better grammar than my dad. I think it bothers her when he doesn't use good grammar. She had a chance to marry another man who became a pastor, and I think that would have been a better fit for her as she is very religious.

But when dad came back from the war in his uniform, he was very handsome, and he was dating my mom's sister until she found someone else. Then he started dating my mom. Mom was a pretty redhead with a forceful personality, but I don't think she was prepared for life on a farm. Things are better now that we live in town and mom teaches school, but I think they each should have married someone else. Sometimes I hear my dad muttering to himself about my mom, and I worry that maybe they are going to get divorced, but that hasn't happened, so I am thankful for that.

I do appreciate that they get along well when we go on vacation, but it would be nice, God, if you could make them get along better the rest of the year. Sometimes it is pretty quiet at mealtimes, and I don't like the tension. Sometimes at meals we listen to children's stories on the radio like Grimm's fairy tales. Stories like "The Little Match Girl" are often really sad, and we all sit around trying not to cry with lumps in our throats, which makes it hard to eat. Other times we sit in front of the big radio in the living room and listen to funny stories like "Fibber McGee and Molly" or "Maggi Muggins" and her adventures with Mr. McGarrity. I am glad that you gave me a good sense of humor, and sometimes I try to make my parents or siblings laugh when things are stressful.

I love to tell stories, and maybe when I get older, I will write a book. I know that Jesus loved to tell stories too—they are called parables, and sometimes it seemed that people didn't really understand them. That must have been frustrating for Jesus. I have a dollhouse with lots of furniture in it and some plastic dolls. When it is raining and we can't play outside, I play with my dollhouse and make up stories to tell my brothers if they are bored. I try to make up mystery stories to entertain them.

Mostly my brothers like building things with their Meccano sets or with wooden sticks and wheels that fit together. One of my brothers loves taking things apart, but he is not quite as good at putting them back together again. He is always the one who is blamed if something is broken or missing, which isn't really fair. My brothers are twins, so they are often compared to each other. They have to share a small room with a single bed, and they have a tiny closet as well, whereas I have a big room with a double bed. I don't know why my mom didn't switch us around. Maybe because she puts most of her clothes in the closet in my room, plus there is a big table in my room where she puts all the geraniums that she digs up in the fall. I have to say that I don't really like the smell of geraniums. Mom always said that she treated her sons and daughters the same, but I don't think that was always the case. I am glad that you believe in being fair, God. In my mom's family the boys and girls were not treated the same. Her mom favored the boys, and they never had to do any work. It was left to the girls to do everything. Maybe that is why mom always wanted my brothers to do chores as well.

Before my mom was married, her father was quite rich, and every Christmas, the girls would get a new fur coat. I think it was hard for her when our dad wasn't making much money just farming, especially since his land wasn't very good. Mom used to live in one of the largest houses in town, and they actually had a town house and a farmhouse, so they would move between them for summer and winter. She joked that people would say "Fall must be coming because the Dicks family is moving back to town."

It must have been nice to be rich and have a big house, but then my grandfather lost all his money in the 1929 market crash. After he died, my grandma just lived on the main level of their big house. I was always afraid of her. She was a tiny little woman who dressed in black even in summer and never smiled. Sometimes she would come and stay with us, but not for very long. One year when mom and dad were building our house in town, we had to stay with her.

That was the year that I came down with a high fever

and had to stay in bed over Christmas, which was awful. The house had a big curved wooden staircase leading to the upstairs where there were at least six bedrooms. We never went up there, but I had nightmares for years about having to climb up the stairs and face that long, dark hallway. In my dream, I would be in the warm kitchen with my mom and other folks, and my mom would tell me to go and get my teddy bear to show the guests. For some reason, in my dream, the bear would always be upstairs, so I would have to climb the winding, dark staircase. Just as I got to the landing, a witch would jump out at me, and I would fall back into a deep sleep. That nightmare is still the beginning of many of my dreams even now, years later. But now that I know I can trust you, God, I just start to pray that you will help me to wake up from bad dreams. In my dreams, I start to blink my eyes as I know that will wake me up, and it does. I am so thankful that you gave me that idea, God, because now I have a way to escape when I have a bad dream.

But back to my family. I want to thank you for my brothers because they are such fun to hang out with, especially because I don't really have friends. I love my little sister, but we are seven years apart, so it is not as much fun to play with her. Besides, I am more of a tomboy and like more active play with my brothers. One of my favorite books was called *The Boxcar Children*. It is about four children who were orphans and had to survive on their own; not that my brothers and I were orphans, but we seemed to band together and spend more time with each other than we did with our parents.

And, dear God, thank you so much for Pop. He is my dad's father, and he has always lived with us ever since my mom and dad got married. My mom and dad work hard, and they don't have a lot of time to play with us. But Pop is always available. His main job is doing some of the supper preparation as he always peels the potatoes and carrots and puts them in cold water in the sink for mom to cook when she gets home from teaching school. He always wears checked shirts and suspenders to hold his pants up because he has a big belly. I have never seen him in a suit and tie, but he is retired, so he just wears the same thing most days. He likes going for walks and visiting other older men, and sometimes he will take me with him. The older men usually live alone, and we don't get offered any treats. Once a man offered Pop a glass containing a small amount of a golden-brown liquid. Pop accepted it and drank it, but

I knew without him telling me that I was not to tell my mom. Mom is strongly against drinking alcohol. (I don't think she read the verse in Ephesians 9:7 about "drink your wine with a joyful heart.") We never have it in the house and have been told lots of times how bad it is. I think Pop drank the alcohol because he was just being polite, and he didn't want to insult the man.

I know that Jesus made water into wine, so I am a little confused about that. Also, the Bible says in 1 Timothy 5:23, "Stop drinking only water, and use a little wine because of your stomach and your frequent illnesses." But in our church, when we have communion, we use grape juice instead of real wine. I hope you are okay with that, God, as I don't think the church is going to change any time soon. And I know my mom is not going to change her opinion either. She never talks about certain Bible verses or about Jesus turning water into wine. I don't remember seeing anyone drunk. I do remember once we were at a wedding, and my mom kept dancing with my Auntie Denise whom we hardly ever saw. I thought my mom was just being kind to her, but later I found out that my aunt had been drinking, and my mom didn't want the other guests to notice.

But back to Pop. In the summer, he takes me to pick berries. We put them in our big honey tins. He doesn't mind if wasps crawl on his hands when he is picking the berries as he says they won't hurt him. Sometimes when we go picking berries, we get pretty far from home, but that doesn't bother Pop. We just go out to the road, and he waits for a car to come along to hitch a ride. He is a big man, and he stands in the middle of the road so the driver really can't miss us and has to slow down, or he would hit Pop. He knows almost everyone in town, so he never worries about getting a lift. Once when I was walking home from school, a man stopped his car and asked if I wanted a lift. I told him that I was not allowed to accept rides from strangers. I found out later that he was a friend of Pop's, and they had a good laugh about it.

I love Pop probably the best of everyone in my family. He is always in a good mood. People say that fat people are jolly, and he is really jolly. I have never heard him criticize anyone or say anything rude. He doesn't go to church, but he can sing the old gospel songs that he listens to on the radio like "When the Roll Is Called up Yonder" or "Shall We Gather at the River." He acts more like a Christian than some of the people that do go to church. He listens to some programs on his radio that I like to hear too, but they are on past my bedtime. Sometimes I take my pillow and lie down in front of his bedroom door. He is a little deaf, so he has the radio turned up high so I can hear the stories pretty well. One was called "Through the Green Door," and it opened with the sound of a door creaking, which was a little scary.

I don't see my dad much as he has a long drive into work every day and gets home really tired. My mom is really strict, and as I said, I respect her, but I don't know about really loving her. But I know that Pop and my siblings love me, and I love them, and that brings me great joy.

Chapter 19

REBECCA NEEDS GOD'S HELP WITH HER STUDIES

Dear God,

Well, it is almost exam time again, and I really need help with history. I just can't seem to memorize all those dates! I am fine with math, and sometimes my teacher will ask me to solve a problem on the blackboard, which I love to do even though I know the other kids think I am being a smarty pants. Learning new things is just so exciting.

But history is so boring! I didn't know what I was going to do about the upcoming history exam, but you gave me this great idea last week. Just before the final exam, our teacher said that, if we wanted him to write up some sample essays on any topic at all, he would do that.

I asked him to write up four essays on some topics that you just put into my head, and he did as he had promised.

And guess what? Well, those were the essays that were on the exam, and I had just finished memorizing them the night before. Thank you so much for helping me with that exam. It is the last time that I have to take history because I am going to take more science courses when I go to high school.

I do like studying art, and once I drew pictures of my brothers when we were on one of our long car rides. I know that you like art because you made such beautiful things in nature. I love that Bible verse in Psalm 19:1 "The heavens declare the glory of God: the skies proclaim the work of His hands."

My mom loves drawing with pastels, which are like colored chalk and quite dusty to work with. She painted two large pictures in our living room that have gold-painted frames. I don't really think they are all that great, but I wouldn't dare say that to her. The daughter of one of her friends was a talented painter, and mom thought I should take lessons from her. I wanted to learn to do oil painting, and Mom bought me a canvas and a set of paints that I loved. I remember one of the colors was called "gentian blue." Isn't that just such a cool description, God? The lady asked me what I wanted to paint, and I said I wanted to paint a sunset over water. Looking back, I think that was probably too difficult for a beginner's oil painting as I had to get rays of sun glinting off the waves. I don't remember what happened to that painting, but I did paint a cat and also our dog, Ginger. I tried some other crafts, but I wasn't really a big fan of handiwork. But being in a 4-H sewing club, I had to knit a wool sweater. Unfortunately, I made the neck really tight, so it was hard to pull over my head— sort of like the skirt that had a waist that was too small. All in all, I'm not much for crafts.

Chapter 20

REBECCA TALKS TO GOD ABOUT CHORES

Hello again, God.

Well, I know that chores are just a part of life, but sometimes that seems unfair as well. I know that, when Adam and Eve got banished from the Garden of Eden, they had to start doing chores—no more wandering around picking tasty fruit. My brothers and I have to do a lot of the inside chores because my dad is always working on something outside in his shop, and my mom likes to work in her garden.

We all have to make our beds in the morning, which is fine, and then we have to do the dishes after each meal. My brothers and I take turns—one washes the dishes and the other dries the dishes. The towels get wet pretty quickly, and sometimes it deteriorates into my brothers flicking wet towels at each other for fun. I hate using wet towels, and when I have my own house, I am just going to let the dishes air dry in the dish drainer. I read somewhere that it is actually more sanitary to do that, but mom likes the dishes dried and put away so the kitchen looks nice and clean. We clean the counter too except for the little space just inside the door where my dad keeps important mail, like bills. He has a little section in the cupboard for his things, but my mom has an actual desk in their bedroom. On the weekends, the three of us kids also have to dust and vacuum the whole house. The dusting is not too bad. We just spray Pledge on a rag and dust away. But the vacuuming is harder because the vacuum doesn't really pick up the dirt very well. Our biggest chore in summer is weeding the garden. We always have to do that before we get time to play. We have a really big garden, and we all have to spend time getting it ready. When we first started to make the garden years ago, the soil was very poor, and there were lots of stones. We had to pick up stones and put them onto a big wooden slab called a stone boat made of logs tied together. A tractor had to pull it onto the garden and then, when it was filled with stones, pull it back off.

Then we hauled in good black soil, which was better for growing things, and the garden was ready for planting.

Once we didn't need the stone boat anymore, we used it as a raft when the spring rains came, but it didn't float very well, so it could hold only one person. Pop made us another raft from a huge tractor tire tube and some wood slats. It was tricky with my two brother and me and only two rafts, so sometimes we got a "boot full" of water while we tried to balance on a small island of grass while we waited for our turn.

Chapter 21

REBECCA IS THANKFUL FOR BOOKS

Dear God,

I am so pleased that you helped people to invent books. I love reading, and it is a great way to escape into other worlds. I love reading about doctors and nurses, and maybe I will be a nurse someday. The doctors in the books always look so handsome and brave. I love reading books about nurses who fall in love with the doctors that they are working with.

Pop has a big bookshelf with lots of books on it, and I can choose from those. He has whole series of books about poor people overcoming difficulties in life (like *Phil the Fiddler*) and loads of Western novels by Zane Gray. Once I asked him about a book that had a picture of a woman on the front, and he said he thought it was probably okay if I read that one. It was actually about a woman who had several husbands (except I don't think they called them husbands in the book), but I remember reading in John 4 that Jesus talked to the woman at the well who had five husbands and explained things to her, so I guess you love everyone even if they make some bad decisions.

I especially love reading my own little Bible. It has a black leather cover that zips up to protect the pages, which are very thin, and when I turn the pages, they make a crinkly sound, which I love. It makes them seem so old and valuable, which they are because it is your love letter to us. It has a few pictures in it—my favorite is one of Jesus talking to the little children. I remember he told the disciples to bring the little children to him so he could bless them. That would have been so exciting. I would have liked to have been one of those children sitting on his knee.

Chapter 22

REBECCA LOVES CHRISTMAS

Dear God,

Christmas is the most exciting day of the year. I know you must love it because it is when Jesus was born. Although it turns out he wasn't born in the wintertime on December 25 when we celebrate it. The weather doesn't get that cold over in Israel, and I was reading that he was likely born much earlier in the year. Plus, the wise men didn't come until Jesus was about two years old because Mary and Joseph were living in a house by then, not in the stable. But our crèche has all the shepherds and the wise men together with Mary, Joseph, baby Jesus, and the animals. I guess it is okay, but I wonder sometimes if people just didn't read the Bible very well. But I am learning that no one likes to be criticized, so I don't share that with anyone.

I have so much fun at Christmas getting gifts for everyone. One year I had $6 to buy for six people. I always get Pop a box of chocolates with maraschino cherries, and my dad a new handkerchief. I got my mom a new pink plastic dustpan as the other one was getting rusty. I got my brothers little cars and my sister a book. My little sister was too young to spend money on Christmas gifts, so she just wrapped up our own toys and put them under the tree for us. One brother said, "Hey this is my Tommy Tractor book!" and she was upset. I think she hoped he would pretend it was something new, but boys aren't good at doing that. Another time my other brother got our mom a Mother's Day card that read, "To someone who has been like a mother to me." I think she just laughed it off. We got our best Christmas gift the year we got our dog, Ginger. Mom and Dad had put a big red bow on him, and he ran into the living room on Christmas morning. That was the only time he was allowed in the living room. One Christmas, my dad got a movie camera, and he filmed us opening our Christmas gifts. Dad loved taking photos, and he really loved his movie camera. But one time when we were on vacation in California, Dad forgot to take out the reel and turn it over to record on the other side. We had a tour of Hollywood and Sea World in Los Angeles, but when he showed the film later, it showed dolphins jumping out of the fountains on the lawns of the movie stars. Dad was really angry at himself. At least he was pretty good about taking interesting shots. Mom used the movie camera sometimes too. I remember she was trying to get a shot of a wild partridge on the side of the road, and she kept the camera trained on a bush for ages before we saw a glimpse of brown feathers that quickly disappeared. Dad was funny about his slides as well. He always wanted to tell us what was just out of sight of the slide we were looking at, so he would say, "Just to the right of the picture [which we couldn't see] was such and such." Dad was also more focused on scenery than people, and especially flowers even though we could have looked at photos of flowers in books more easily. But besides music and games, showing slides to guests was our entertainment because we didn't have a TV. Playing games was fun because the children were included with the adults in all the games. I especially like Rummoli, but we used toothpicks instead of poker chips because that would be too much like gambling, which was not allowed. One section of the game was labeled Poker Pot, but we never played that. But it was fun to see the toothpick piles getting higher and higher when no one would have an ace-king or a 7-8-9 card combination to play. We were so excited you would think we were playing for real money.

Speaking of games, Pop liked to play cribbage with me, and that was helpful in terms of learning math. Pop also liked to do jigsaw puzzles, and he made himself a large board for the one-hundred and two-hundred-piece puzzles that he kept on his dresser. He worked on them when he had nothing else to do.

Chapter 23

REBECCA THANKS GOD FOR BIRTHDAYS

I love birthdays, and we usually celebrate with my Aunts' families. Mom would sometimes make a special two-layer birthday cake and wrap pennies, nickels, and dimes in waxed paper and put them in between the layers before she iced the cake so when we were eating our slice, we might find some money. Luckily nobody ever swallowed any money.

Once we started traveling in the summer, we were always away on my birthday because it is near the end of July, and that was when my dad took his two weeks of holidays. Once Mom made delicious chocolate squares called Nanaimo bars that we took along, but it got so hot that they started to melt, so we had to eat more of them than usual. That was fine with me as they were my favorites. Another time I remember that Mom gave me a two-dollar bill for my birthday and apologized that it was all she could manage that year. Maybe that was one of the years that hail destroyed my dad's crops. I think that was also why my mom returned to teaching school; farming was so unpredictable. All your hard work slaving away could be destroyed in a matter of ten minutes, and then you would have no money to see you through the next year. Eventually my dad decided to become a welder, and that was steady work despite a long commute. He would be so tired at the end of the day, he would just lie down for a rest until it was time for supper.

When I got older and money wasn't such a problem, I got an allowance. I would save a dime for the collection at Sunday school, and then I would walk to the store to buy candy with the rest. I like most candy except for licorice. Pop always had hard candy to share—funny striped ones called humbugs. My mom said that she always liked caramel toffee, but it was too hard for me to chew. She said she used to buy it when she was younger because it would last such a long time. I was afraid I would crack my teeth on it. I usually chose Cadbury's four flavors, which had vanilla, chocolate, caramel, and maple. One year, I put one dime out of my allowance each week into a piece of cardboard that had little holes in it that were just the size of dimes. It was for a charity called the March of Dimes, and when we filled all the slots, it would be sent to help kids with polio.

I don't remember too much about polio except getting some medicine on a little cube of sugar at school. I only knew one person who had polio, and she was one of my mom's relatives. Once my mom took me to visit her in the hospital, and she was in a long metal tube that made a hissing sound with air going in and out. They called it an iron lung. You could see her face in the mirror above her head, but she couldn't move the rest of her body, which was in the long tube. It was so sad, but it made me want to be a nurse even more so I could help sick people.

Chapter 24

REBECCA LOVES GOD

Dear God,

I just wanted to tell you how much I love you and how safe and secure I feel knowing that you are always there looking after me.

Sometimes it is hard for me to know what you want me to do in certain situations. At times like that, I just pray and ask you to give me a sense of your presence inside me. I don't know about other people, but sometimes when I pray, I have an excited feeling in my stomach as if you are saying, "Hello. I'm here anytime you need me."

Sometimes when I am looking for your help, I just open my Bible anywhere and read the first line that I see. I know some people think that is not a good way to find out what your will is, but sometimes it seems that you just guide me to the exact Bible passage that I need to read. I hope you are okay with me doing that occasionally. It's like the story in Judges 6 about Jacob putting out the fleece when he wanted your advice about what he should do. And you didn't get annoyed with him when he wasn't sure if you meant it the first time and he tested you again. So, hopefully, you won't be annoyed with me if sometimes I just read a Bible verse at random.

It is hard for me to understand why some people don't believe in you, especially when they look at nature and think about all the stars and galaxies. And when I think about how babies are born and what a miracle that is— those things just can't be replicated by humans. I really don't know how people who don't know you handle difficult situations. They must get so depressed and anxious that they have to look after everything themselves. I am glad I can give that responsibility to you.

I don't know what the future holds for me, but I just pray that you and I will always have a special relationship even when I am an adult. I don't ever want to leave you, and I know you won't ever leave me. I am so glad I can talk to you about everything and anything. I love you.

Yours truly, Rebecca

Printed in the United States
by Baker & Taylor Publisher Services